Kenneth Grahame
The Wind in The Willows

adapted by
Michel Plessix

Vol. 3
The Gates of Dawn

NANTIER · BEALL · MINOUSTCHINE
Publishing inc.
new york

Also available:
The Wind in the Willows:
volumes 1,2: $15.95 each
The Princess & The Frog: $15.95
The Fairy Tales of Oscar Wilde:
volumes 1,2,3: $15.95 each
The Fairy Tales of the Brothers Grimm: $15.95
Jungle Book: $16.95
Peter and the Wolf: $15.95

(add $3 P&H first item, $1 each addt'l)

We have over 150 graphic novels available
write for our color catalog:
NBM, Dept. S
185 Madison Ave., Ste. 1504
New York, NY 10016

ISBN 1-56163-245-7
©1999 Guy Delcourt Productions / Plessix
©1999 NBM for the English translation
Translation by Joe Johnson
Lettering by Ortho
Printed in France

5 4 3 2 1

Chapter VII

The Piper at the Gates of Dawn

It was ten-thirty on a summer's eve...Almost the title of a novel, thought the Mole.

The day still hadn't gotten used to the idea that it was time to come to a close. Yet it had exerted itself greatly with its friend the sun, both doing far more than their duty...The afternoon had been oppressive, stifling, overpowering. In short, it had been horribly hot!

Stretched out in the shade of a willow, the Mole had spent it contemplating the despairingly absent clouds, listening to the buzzing concert of the insects.

Buzzing and endless...

How ever could one be so active in such weather?

The Mole was at this advanced stage in his existential reflections when a light footfall on the parched grass startled him.

FRITCHHH!

1

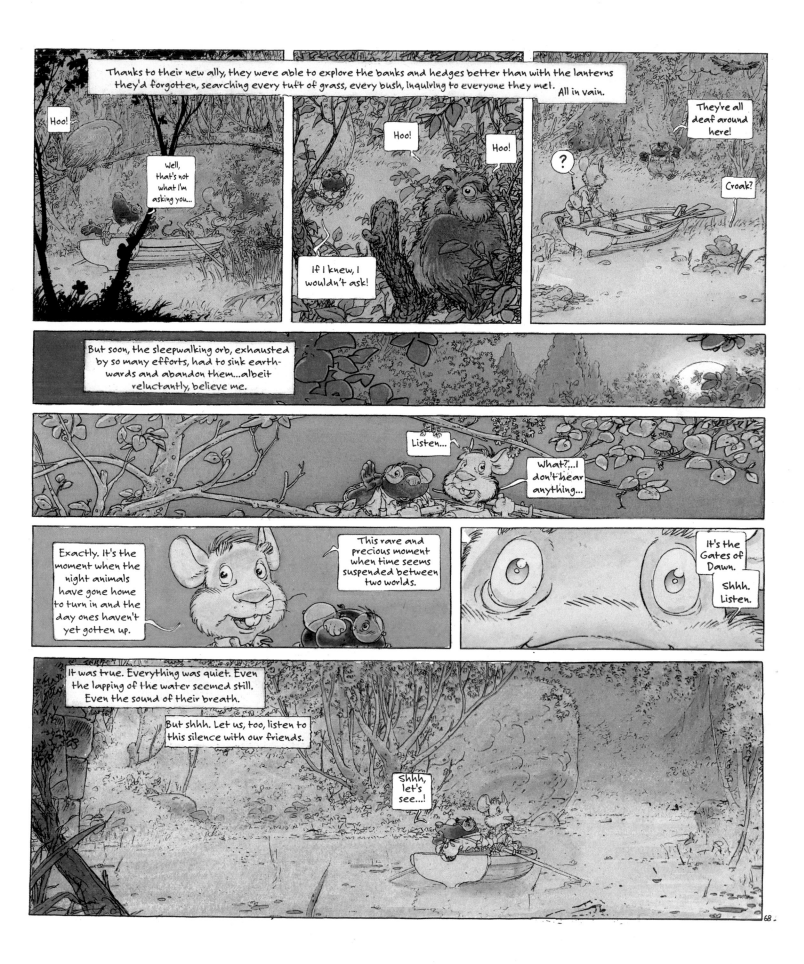

Thanks to their new ally, they were able to explore the banks and hedges better than with the lanterns they'd forgotten, searching every tuft of grass, every bush, inquiring to everyone they met. All in vain.

Hoo!

Well, that's not what I'm asking you...

Hoo!

Hoo!

If I knew, I wouldn't ask!

?

They're all deaf around here!

Croak?

But soon, the sleepwalking orb, exhausted by so many efforts, had to sink earthwards and abandon them...albeit reluctantly, believe me.

Listen...

What?...I don't hear anything...

Exactly. It's the moment when the night animals have gone home to turn in and the day ones haven't yet gotten up.

This rare and precious moment when time seems suspended between two worlds.

It's the Gates of Dawn.

Shhh. Listen.

It was true. Everything was quiet. Even the lapping of the water seemed still. Even the sound of their breath.

But shhh. Let us, too, listen to this silence with our friends.

Shhh, let's see...!

68

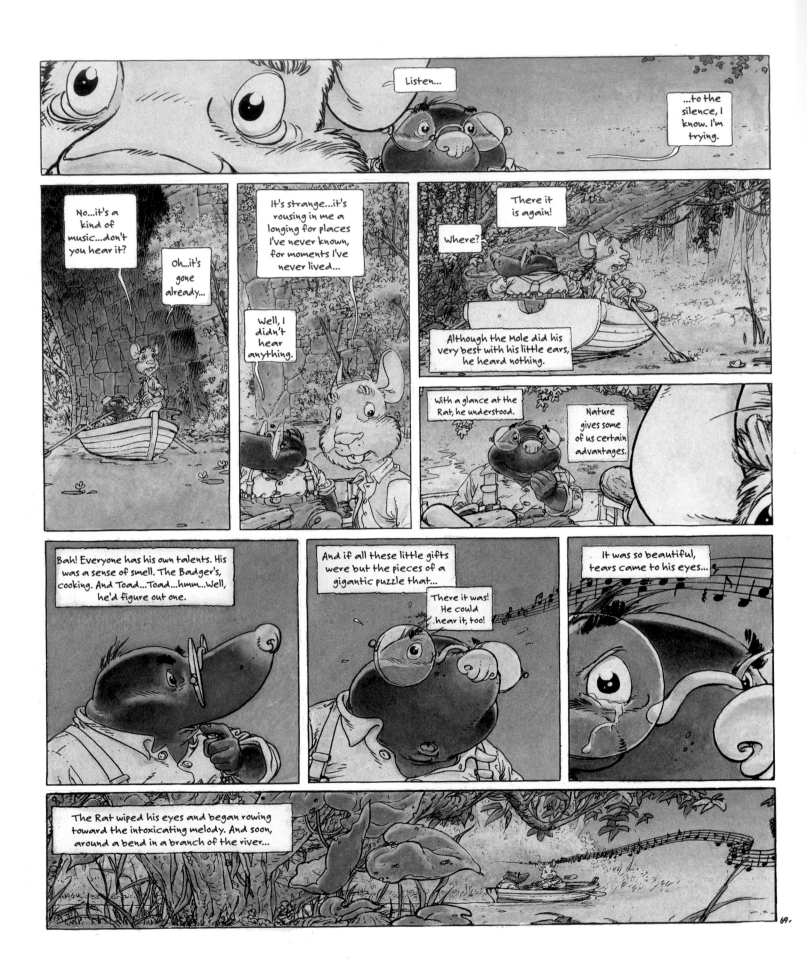

It seemed to be coming from there, from that small island bordered with willows and silvered birches. Something irresistible drew them there.

They landed without incident. The ground was carpeted with fragrant flowers and soft, thick moss.

They followed a sort of pathway between the wild fruit-trees. The Mole was so agitated that he didn't even think of gorging himself.

The music had stopped. The Mole, too. Everything now seemed utterly silent. It seemed to him that some terrible and beautiful Presence was near. Something that demanded awe and respect, that he would doubtless never again see.

So, slowly, humbly, the Mole dared to lift his eyes.

He looked in the very eyes of the Friend and Helper. A shiver ran through him.

The little animals remained dazed and dumbfounded. They felt as though they had the dim afterthought of an uncertain memory...

It was as though they'd awakened from a beautiful dream, already fading despite the struggle to recall, leaving only a profound, serene feeling of wellbeing.

Hello? Some great animal has been here...

I wonder where he went...the island is so little...

Huh?! A beast? Where??

Aah! Something moved over there!

Where?

There, I tell you!

It seems pretty small to have left such big tracks...

Little Portly!

Well, you can brag that you had us worried, you little scamp!

You know, I wasn't afraid!

I'd never seen him before, but, I don't know why, I'd have recognized him right away.

While leaving the island, the Mole couldn't stop himself from turning back one final time, full of an incomprehensible sadness, and from contemplating this place that, he didn't know why, would always be part of him.

We won't linger over the intimacy of the reunion of father and son, and like the Mole and Rat, let's distance ourselves discreetly.

So! There you are?!

And your mother? Did you think of your poor mother?

23.

10

Chapter VII

Toad's Adventures

When she entered, a delicious fragrance filled both the room and Toad's nostrils.

It smelled of fragrant tea, warm apples, toast and muffins coated in melting butter dripping with the colors of honey.

It was clear! She was going to try to seduce him through his stomach...A classic feminine technique...

That was making little ado of his famous strength of character!

What a crude stratagem! Ha! Never would a frog worthy of the name let himself be trapped so easily!

KS KSS KSS

YUM
SCRUNCH GOBBLE
BURP SMACK CRUNCH
GORGE GLOOP

hee hee

I knew you weren't so difficult...

Until tomorrow?

15

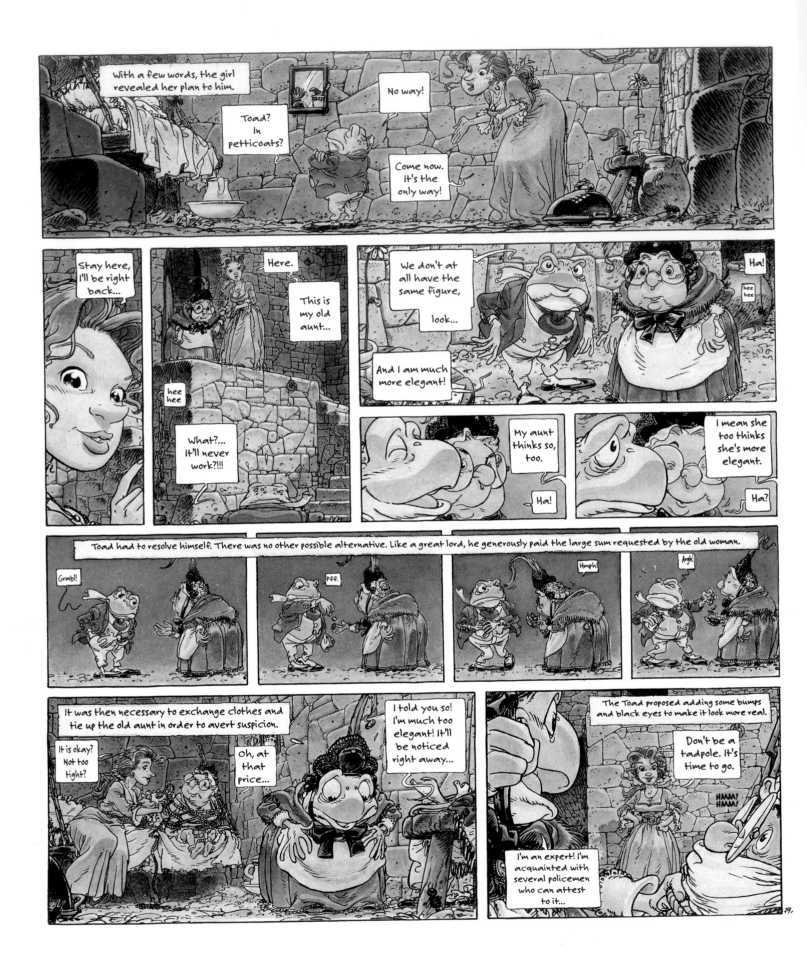

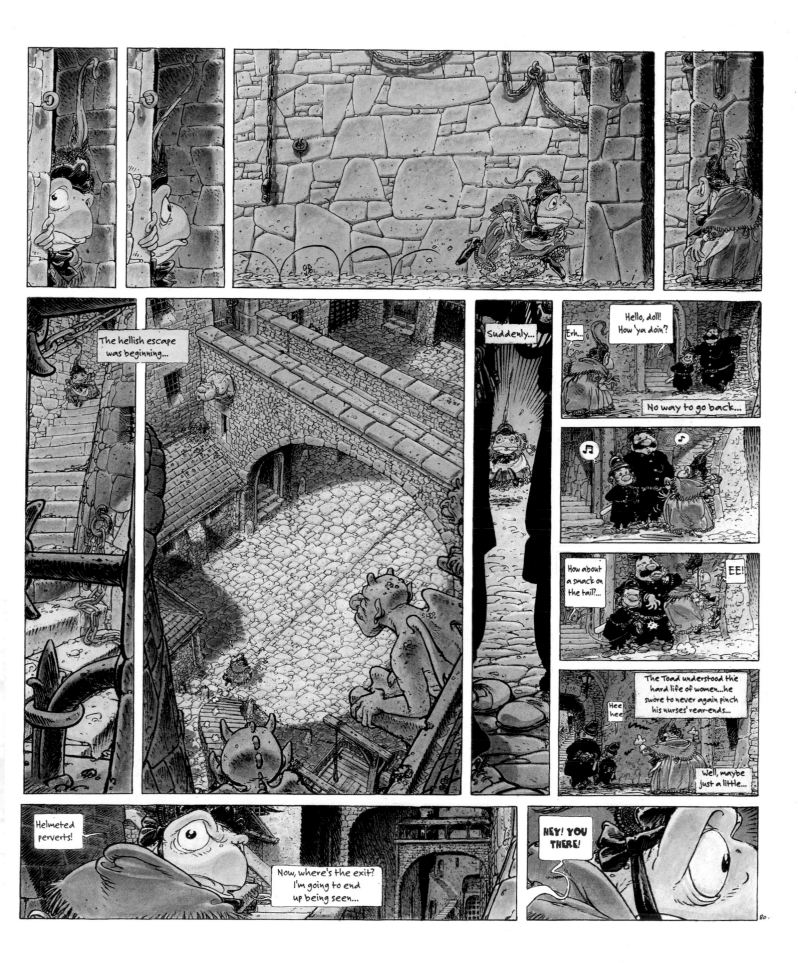

21

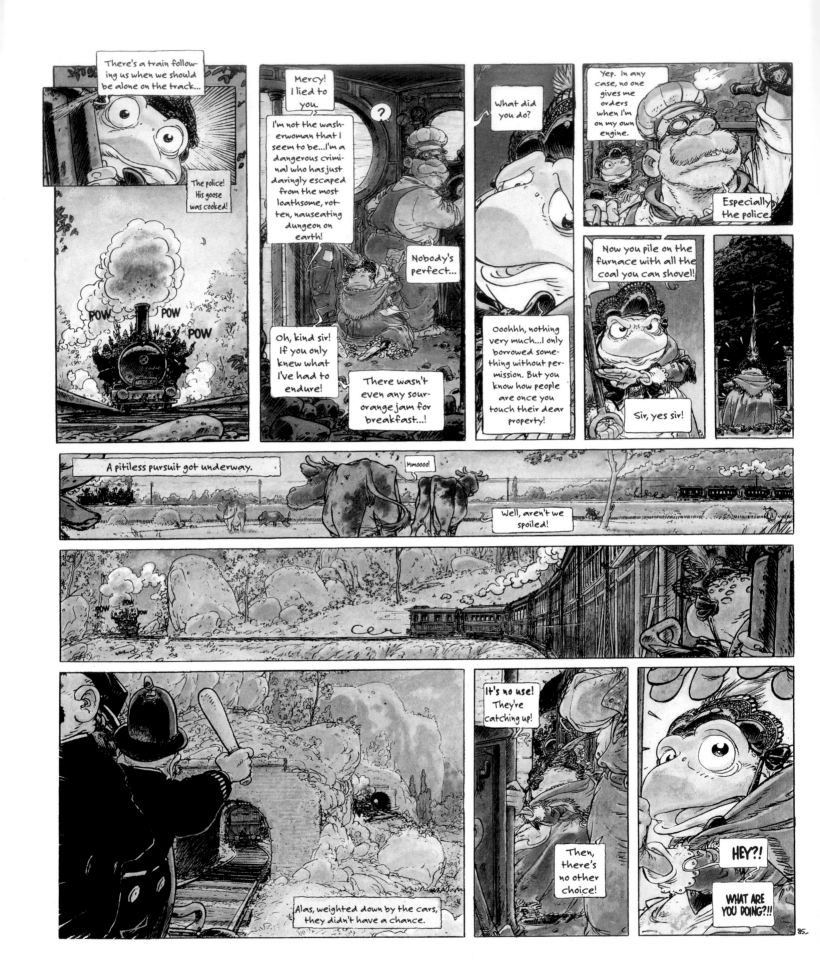

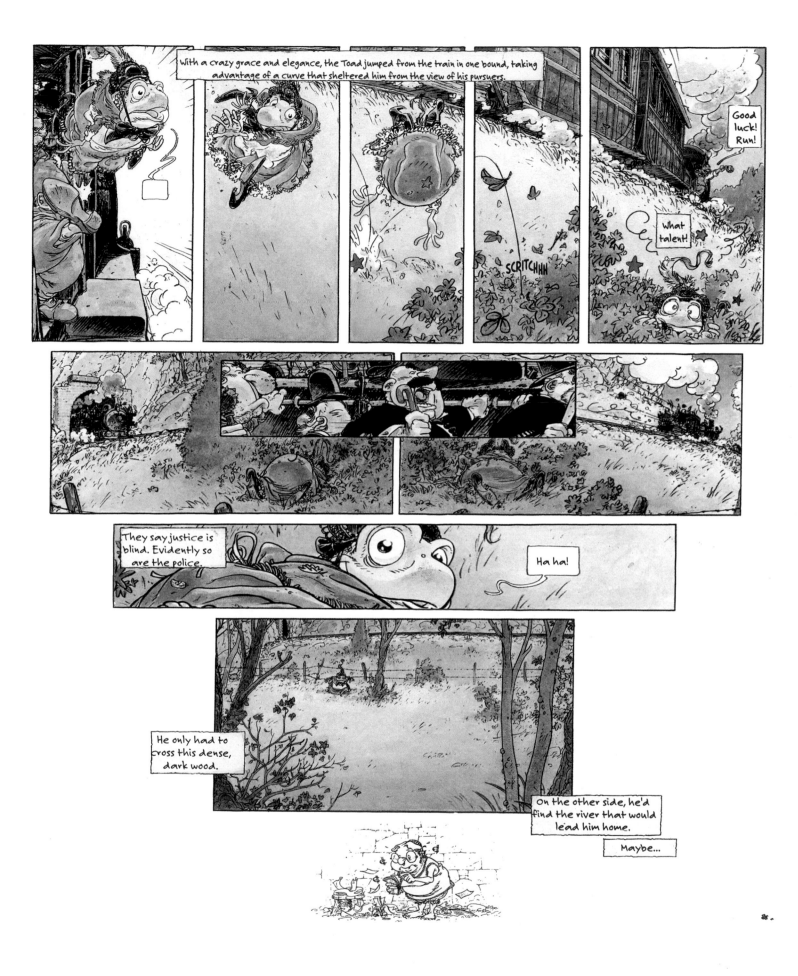

Chapter IX

The Further Adventures of Toad

27

Will Toad die drowned at
the bottom of the river ?

Will he become shellfish and eel food ?

What are those strange silhouettes which have
apparently invaded Toad Hall ?

Will the porcupines
finally go to school ?

What are our
beweaponed friends
doing in this mysterious
secret tunnel ?

Why must every thing
finish violently?

Will all these questions find answers in the next volume.

Well it better, 'cause it'll be the last!

michel Ressin — January 98
June 99   -Essaouira, Tinos, Le Pigeonnier du chapitre, Etables s/mer